IMPURE

LICHIGAN

Sword and Sorcery from the Great Lakes Realm

THE FIRST TALE:
Don't Drink the Water in Firestone

Connor Coyne

GOTHIC FUNK PRESS

Flint, Michigan

GOTHIC FUNK PRESS

gothicfunkpress.com

Flint, Michigan

IMPURE LICHIGAN:

SWORD AND SORCERY FROM THE GREAT LAKES REALM

THE FIRST TALE:

DON'T DRINK THE WATER IN FIRESTONE

Copyright © 2022 by Connor Coyne

Designed and Illustrated by **Sam Perkins-Harbin**

forge22.com

ISBN: 978-1-956722-06-2

Printed in the United States of America.

10 9 8 7 6 5 4 3 2 1

First Edition

for Dad
who introduced me to books
about unbelievable situations
and very believable people

♟

On a spell-bitten night, at the waning of the year, when the mums were in bloom and rotting apples spiced the air, Shalm set out to fetch a flagon of mead from the Lantern.

This was her ritual of penance. Her punishment. Pain and pleasure, nectar bridged. When duty calls, honor bids us answer, but Shalm appreciated above all the tenderness with which honey sweetness harrowed the bitterness of need. Even if smoke and twilight merged and became fire-breathing dragons, she'd cleave them if they came between herself and her destination.

Nine-hundred-and-seventy-five turns of the wagon wheel carried her to the battered gates of the City of Firestone. From there, it was another one-thousand-one-hundred-and-twenty-one steps on the rain-slicked cobbles to bring her to the dirt treads of the Serpent's Alley in the Tavern District. Another sixty-three steps carried her to the margins of the Lantern. Shalm had only been coming to Firestone for two months, but already this watering hole felt comfortable and familiar. True, the two torches ensconced above the entrance tarred the night with smoke, and a reek came up from the hoppish puddles underfoot, but the laughter that fell through that door spoke a reassuring lie of comfort and companionship, and she smelled mead, too. Shalm could almost see it suffusing the atmosphere like a fine mist of clover pollen.

Tonight, however, something was different. A long line of humanity emerged from the bowels of the tavern and snaked its way back up the alley. There must have been at least a hundred souls, not counting the children capering about their mothers' knees. The Lantern was popular at the changing of the guard, but Shalm had never seen a line outside. Not like this. Not on a Dawnday.

"What?" she asked a skinny man waiting outside the entrance. "A fortune teller? A drover hiring? What?"

The man stared at her uncomprehendingly.

"Bah!" she said and shoved past him. She had already been a long day desheathing corn, and Shalm wasn't about to spend her evening waiting for a fool to speak.

"Hey!" the man called after her. "Mind the line! I've been waiting out here for four spans!"

Shalm climbed the seven stairs and slammed the door behind her.

Inside, more torches exhaled more smoke. All the tables were full, as were the spaces between the tables. The line from outside broke against the stone walls like the waves of an impatient sea and sprayed its constituents among the wooden floorboards. What Shalm had mistaken for laughter was today a sore complaint.

"Mead!" shouted the old men. "Mead!" shouted the mothers. "Mead!" shouted their grime-footed children.

"Mead!" shouted Shalm.

"There'll be no mead," came a soft voice at her side.

Shalm looked down at the speaker. It was a tiny woman with lively eyes. She had skin the color of umber, an alert posture, and her hair, black with streaks of steel, was pulled back in a severe bun. Yet there was something charming and mischievous about the woman. She looked like a sorceress, though not a very frightening one. Indeed, the burlap robe was a full cord too big for her, and she kept pulling the sleeves up over her hands. She shook her head, lifted a steaming mug to her lips, and took a sip.

"No mead?" asked Shalm.

"None," said the awkward woman. "For you or for them."

"Why not?" Shalm asked.

She didn't ask this in a friendly or a curious way. She wanted to *impose* upon the diminutive speaker. Shalm knew how to impose. Her skin was so pale white, her eyes so dark and brooding, that she often seemed bloodless with anger. Her icy scorn seemed as ageless as glaciers and as sharp as icicles, though Shalm had scarcely known four decades in this land. True, she wasn't the tallest soul in the Lantern that night, but she was taller than most. She weighed more than most men and could sprawl across two full chairs when she had the mind. She could also sprawl a drunken lout upon his face with a flash of her fist. No, when Shalm *imposed,* it was with a silent anger, a perceived edge, a steady-breath awareness that *imposed* the spirit of danger upon those who stood about her. *This woman has acted in violence,* they thought. *This woman has injured those who opposed her.*

But the little would-be sorceress slurped from her mug and didn't seem to notice any imposition whatsoever.

"What about you?" asked Shalm. "You seem to have plenty of mead."

"No mead for me," said the woman. "I'm drinking tea."

The conversation seemed to have hit a dead end, and Shalm wasn't sure why she had spoken to this berobed woman in the first place. She turned her back and forced her way to the stone table where the tavernkeeper shouted against his innumerable guests.

"We need mead!" they cried.

"I've got no more mead!" he cried back.

"Mead! Mead!"

"What do you mean you're out of mead?" asked Shalm. "You're a mead hall!"

He flinched when she spoke. Shalm had no trouble imposing upon the tavernkeeper. *He* would answer her.

"The water!" he said.

"The water?"

"It's been corrupted. Haven't you heard?"

"Clearly, I have not."

"Ever since the Lich ascended, he's been driving us hard

with sanctions, scarcities, and scarifications. He says we're too thin, and that we do not render our tithe!"

"So?"

"He told his servants not to cast the purification spells on the river. He never told us of these privations. We've been drinking it these past eighteen months. It's ensorceled. It's contaminated. It's deadly!"

"Mead!" roared the crowd. "We need mead!" they pleaded.

"What do I care about the water?" asked Shalm. "I'm here for *mead*!"

"So is everyone else!" explained a milkmaid wearing a grimy frock. "The mead doesn't come in from the river! They barrel it up in Dire Straits and cart it here on the week. The mead is safe to drink!"

"Yes," said the tavernkeeper. "And I tell you all; you've drunk me dry."

"Have we?" Shalm asked in a deadly voice, and her eyes met the tavernkeeper's.

She saw his glance flicker, a subtle movement downward. It only lasted an instant, but Shalm understood. Without taking her eyes off him, she leaned over the table and reached for the shelf beneath. Shalm's hand found the clay handle of a small flagon, and she lifted it over the counter. With her other hand, she felt for a coin in her belt pouch, but her greatsword kept getting in the way. It was a massive weapon, and it jangled in its scabbard. Shalm didn't hear the sound of the angry angler behind her lifting a wooden stool over his head. She saw his shadow cross the torchlight, however. She started to turn – too late! – but a robed hand shot out and shoved the falling stool aside. It missed Shalm's head, shattering the flagon instead. A spray of mead erupted from the wreckage, covering the stone table, the tavernkeeper, the angler, the milkmaid, and the milkmaid's three children, who started licking the sticky liquid from their arms.

Shalm didn't bother with her sword. Her hand found the hilt of a small, wickedly-curved dagger, and she leveled it toward the angler.

"I wanted that," she said.

But combat had been joined elsewhere.

"You're holding out on us!" shrieked the milkmaid, lunging at the tavernkeeper, who fell back with a wail. The angler turned his back on Shalm and started rooting under the table in case there was another hidden flagon of mead. The boiling crowd, stomping their feet, lifting their fists, jumping upon every stool and every table, smelling the fresh mead in the air, the delicious mead, the *drinkable* mead, converged upon the table. They got in each other's way, and when they couldn't get where they were going, they started hitting and kicking and gouging and biting whoever was nearest.

But there was no more mead. Shalm had found the last flagon. Now that it had been destroyed, the crowd's violence of desire had become the violence of atavism. And Shalm had no use for atavism. No, there was nothing for her here tonight. She wiped her arms dry with a discarded towel and shouldered her way back toward the murky alley. She heard the sounds of fists and shouts diminishing behind her. As she climbed down the seven steps into the alley, she didn't notice a little woman in enormous robes following her.

2

As it went with the Lantern, so it went with the Cellar, the Eyrie, and Lord Conquest's Inn. Shalm took the rickety footbridge across the river, but the Mellowmarsh Tavern was bereft of mead. So was the Scarrèd Rock. She even ducked briefly into the foggy antechamber of the Moist Magician, but one look at the irritable fops arguing over the scarcity of bees in October told her that there was no mead here. The district's stores of cider, wine, and beer had been similarly annihilated.

The cursed water drawn from the river was worse than unfit for drinking. Only half-cured as it sat in the cisterns, it now threw fell spells into the lungs and the brain, hurting and killing unwary quaffers. A dozen had died, they said, or a half-dozen dozen, and scores of hundreds more knew the scars. But in truth, nobody knew how many had died, how many were diseased, for the Lich had leveled his iron palm and stifled the complaints. All that remained were coffins covered with bland reports of untimely illness, the sludge parents carried to their children for quaffing, the sores and rashes and shed hair that followed encounters with a flagon or trough.

Things had grown dire in Firestone.

Now that her thousands could not draw safe water from their wells, any substitute was sufficient, and Shalm suspected the local heifers and nanny goats were as depleted as the taverns. Perhaps in the morning, the children might step outside with small cloth rags to collect dew and wring it out over their stone drinking basins.

But the night had not yet aged, and Shalm was not the sort of woman to leave any task unfinished. Finishing unfinished tasks was her specialty. No, if there was a single draught of mead left within the city of Firestone, she meant to find it. A ritual of penance is not easily laid aside. A punishment cannot be abrogated by the preference of convenience. And so, Shalm crisp-stepped the damp flagstones, her thoughts turned toward the outer districts, and what inconspicuous dirt-floored taverns might have escaped the notice of the mob.

Something else had also started to impress itself upon her brain. Shalm was being followed. Oh, she had doubted for a while, for the streets were still thick with nobles and merchants in their thirsty efforts to shed the day's salt. But counting her steps from one tavern to the next, Shalm became aware of a padded, mincing footfall about thirty paces behind her. As suspicion hardened into certainty, Shalm resisted the temptation to look over her shoulder and betray her awareness. She waited until she was approaching the Scarrèd Rock from the east. It had a bank of new windows, and the owners scrubbed them weekly. Lifting her eyes to look in the glass, Shalm momentarily saw, reflected among the other figures coming and going, the little woman in the voluminous robes.

Smiling inwardly at her discovery, Shalm made no answer but continued along her path. After the disappointment at the Moist Magician, she quickened her pace, slipped around the corner of the Turtles' Alley, and waited near the wall, dagger drawn. A moment later, the berobed woman appeared and found herself face-to-face with a scowling Shalm. The curved dagger seemed to glow in the lamplight.

"Hello," said the woman.

"Why are you following me?" asked Shalm.

"I didn't have anything else to do." The woman frowned. "I didn't have anywhere else to go."

This didn't seem like much of an answer. Shalm raised her dagger threateningly.

"My name is Jayn," said the little woman. "I get bored sometimes. I look for something to do. You seemed an interesting person. You were asking for mead, and not because you wanted water, and not because you wanted to get drunk. No, you have some other purpose in your mind. I wondered about this. I decided to follow you because I wanted to learn more about you."

"You shouldn't follow people," said Shalm. "They feel

threatened. Threatened people do dangerous things."

"I'm sorry if I offended you. I just get so curious sometimes. Asking questions and answering them is my whole life. It is the only thing I really enjoy, but I enjoy it tremendously."

Shalm didn't answer.

"My name is Jayn," Jayn repeated.

Shalm grunted.

She took a seat on a boulder that offered a prospect of the muddy streets. Jayn grinned and sat beside her.

"You aren't going to find any mead in Firestone tonight," she said.

"Maybe in the outer districts," said Shalm.

"Not even there. I live in an outer district. Every bottle, every flagon, every basin is empty. When the water turns bad, people drink what they can."

"I've got to try."

"The Lich hasn't prohibited trying. Yet."

Shalm got to her feet.

"Don't follow me," she said.

"Actually, I was wondering if I could just walk with you this time. Instead of following."

Shalm sighed and started off in the direction of the Great

Red Road.

"May I walk with you?" Jayn called after her.

"The Lich hasn't prohibited walking. Yet."

They made their way south. The carriages and wagons were only now starting to clear the streets. Firestone had an evil reputation after dark, and if the peasants had poached all the potables, it'd be an early night indeed. Still, Shalm had one last card to play. She knew of a tavern in the City of the Sun District, not far from the encircling walls. The Copper Chalice. It carried a big crowd when the caravans were moving, but on a Dawnday, it would be quieter than any drinkery in the Tavern District. If a drop of mead was to be found anywhere in Firestone, it would be at the Copper Chalice.

Seventy-three. Seventy-four. Seventy-five. Shalm tried to play the count of her paces from the tavern against her meditation on the Chalice. It was hard here; the Great Red Road turned muddy brown in weather like this, and many of her steps were uneven. And then there was Jayn's voice prattling on somewhere in the mist.

"But that's why I'm so sure," Jayn was saying. "Because they need it."

Shalm realized that she had been ignoring Jayn and wondered if the woman had said anything helpful.

"Who needs it? And what do they need?" Shalm asked.

"The water," Jayn answered. "It isn't like before, when the

refuse was sitting out in the middle of the street or when the great fires raged. Those were fearful things. But water! We need water as certainly as we need air. And the burgomaster said it was safe to drink, as did the overlord. The Lich himself said it was safe to drink, though the vetted scrolls told how he sent his own special caches of water to his deputies here in the city."

"Deputies in the city!" snorted Shalm. "The Lich doesn't have any deputies in this city. He has cursed this city. He won't set foot in Firestone."

"Indeed, you are wrong on that. He himself won't set foot in Firestone, but he has very powerful deputies here, and they live here, and they gaze down on these streets with their red-glowing eyes, but they never come out during the day."

Jayn drew her robes closer around her, staring into the mist as if expecting the red eyes to come floating through the haze like will-o'-the-wisps.

"Why are you searching so hard for mead tonight?" she asked.

One-hundred-and-twenty-seven. One-hundred-and-twenty eight. Shalm ground her teeth, trying to decide if and how to answer. Jayn's cheerful curiosity was grating but effective.

"It's just a tradition of mine," Shalm finally said. "On the first Dawnday following the Hunter's Moon, the weight of my sins courses against me." *Why am I telling her this?* she wondered. It wasn't the kind of confession she usually made. "I set off after dark and drink a flagon of mead alone. That's ordinary enough for a baler of hay. So you see, I am not the fascinating creature that you imagine me to be. You have spent your night following someone mundane and uninteresting."

One-hundred-and-forty-five.

"Oh, I think you're very interesting!"

Now that she had been discovered, Jayn was the spirit of volubility. Shalm tried to ignore Jayn as she spun tales about the Burgomaster Florin and the Nine Magistrates, about the Lich and his deputies. The Road got muddier as they went, and it took all of Shalm's concentration to count the paces she had taken. She knew that if she lost count, she'd be mired in ignorance, and great if inexplicable misfortune might follow. So it had been, and so it would always be. Indeed, the penalty for miscounting might be almost as terrible as that for neglecting her penance. Shalm tried to tamp this fear down and focus on her feet.

Finally, nine-hundred-and-ninety-five steps from the alley, they arrived at a shadowy alcove sheltering the small wooden door to the Copper Chalice. Mead or no mead, the place was closed.

"I told you," said Jayn. "All of the taverns will be closing now. They're all out. Of everything. People need water, and they'll drink whatever they can."

Shalm clenched and unclenched her hands. After hours of wandering, she was starting to worry for the first time. What *would* she do? What if there *wasn't* a drop of mead in the whole city? Would she throttle a noble in the hopes of finding a flask?

"You look tired," said Jayn. "Some root tea will live you up. And I know of an excellent tea house not too far from here."

"How do you drink your tea?" asked Shalm. "If the water is all poisoned?"

It was an obvious question, and she should have asked it sooner.

"I have a cistern," said Jayn. "I cast my own purification spells. Sadly, I must cast them constantly, but they have served me well so far."

"Are you a sorceress?"

Jayn laughed merrily.

"My magics are as small and inconsequential as I am!" she said. "Come with me. I'll buy you a cup of tea, and we'll ruminate profoundly on how to help you fulfill your tradition."

"If the taverns are all closed —"

"The taverns may be closed, but some hearts and eyes are awake. You'll see!"

Jayn turned on her heel and started back toward the heart of the city. Shalm hesitated a moment, then followed.

"Jayn," she said.

"Yes, m'lady?" Jayn answered over her shoulder.

"Call me Shalm," Shalm said.

3

Now that Jayn took the lead, the pace picked up considerably. Shalm realized that she had overestimated the effectiveness of her long gait. Jayn leapt nimbly from puddle to puddle while Shalm loped behind, still struggling to keep count as she went. The two backtracked a full half of their steps together, taking the footbridge over the river for the third time that night, and both the number of Shalm's steps and her surprise exceeded her expectations as they abandoned the well-trod passways of the Tavern District and entered the crumbling labyrinth of the Ruined District. Here hulked wrecked castles, empty except for the bats and bugbears crouching in the corners, waiting to rob and pillage. And yet, while Jayn might have seemed an easy meal for these creatures of the night, they discerned the same threat in Shalm as did the patrons of the Lantern. The way she did not look from side to side yet seemed utterly aware of their lurking presence. The way they didn't seem to cow her in the least.

At length, the unlikely pair emerged onto the fastness of the Great Fording Road, and there Shalm was surprised to see a small golden window glittering in the dark. Smoke piped out of a tin tube on the roof. A heavy iron door barred the way, but Jayn rapped three times on the vast plates, making them ring like a bell. A moment later, a man cracked the door and peered out at Jayn and Shalm with small, suspicious eyes.

"It's late, Jayn," was all he said.

Jayn slipped past him and beckoned Shalm to follow her. They took their seat at a small round table with an ochrish woven tablecloth and a single candle providing most of the light in the room. Somewhere around a corner, a fire smoldered, adding to the sleepy atmosphere.

"I was about to close up," the man said as he closed the door behind him.

"You've had customers tonight?" Jayn asked.

"Zero until now. And now two. What would you like?"

"Use my water," Jayn said. "Mint with milk. For my friend, almond with honey."

The teamaster took the water from Jayn and left the room.

"Is he our answer?" asked Shalm in a low voice.

"Yes," said Jayn. "He makes the best tea in town."

"I don't need tea. I need mead."

"Ah, yes, that. I thought that the tea might clear our minds."

"Is it hallucinogenic tea?"

"Indeed, no. I keep that at my house. But the tea here *is* very good. But worry not; we can talk now while we wait."

Shalm ground her teeth. *Does this woman convolute every thing?*

"Why didn't we discuss this on the way here? The night wears on, and I must have mead by morning."

"We couldn't have talked. I was busy leaping puddles. You were trying to keep track of how many steps we took. Besides, we wouldn't want to speak of deception and intrigue out on the streets where any brigand might hear us."

Shalm glowered.

"What is it, for Mirror's sake?"

"Not so loud!" Jayn hissed in return. "But I do know of someone who I am certain must possess some mead."

"And that is?"

"Lord Mournloff."

Shalm laughed out loud. Once again, Jayn had jested her, although this time at least it looked like she was at least going to get a hot cup of tea out of it. Jayn was, of course, correct: Lord Mournloff would undoubtedly have had mead at his estate, and the finest mead in the realm at that. But in both wealth and prestige, the lord towered about Shalm and Jayn as a giant might have loomed over a gnat. Far from looking down upon them, the good lord wouldn't even deign to notice them. Even the good lord's butler!

"I do not jest," said Jayn.

"Then that tea you've been drinking must have been the magic vision tea you keep at home!"

"Indeed, no, though you should not scorn its visions. Did I not tell you that I was a scrollmaster?"

"Did you?"

"I certainly did, though I suppose it is possible that you were not paying attention as you counted. A great scrollmaster and scholar am I, and as I sift and scribe – matters of deadly spells and infernal impositions – oh, but I come upon many secret things."

"Secret things," repeated Shalm, with emphasis.

"Rumors, mostly. Idle imaginings and false boasts. Delusions. Gossip. Fancy. And, a few true things."

"True things," repeated Shalm.

"Three separate documents, written in three different hands, using alphabets corresponding to three different centuries of the world, all speak of a Silver Sieve created in the Old Days and brought as plunder to Firestone in its beginning. A Silver Sieve whose sorcerous virtue resides in its power *to purify water*!"

Shalm was lost for words. Again she suspected that Jayn was jesting her, but for once, there was no mirth in the scrollmaster's eyes.

"It cannot be," Shalm finally said. "You said that the water was ensorcled. If so, it would take a powerful device to reverse the magic. If the Nine Magistrates had such a device, they would have used it long ago. No, it must have been ruined or destroyed, if it ever existed in the first place."

"It existed. And it exists. The other scrollmasters have spoken of it. Some of them have seen it. Where it is, I do not know. Why the magistrates have not used it, I do not know that either. But if we can retrieve it and gift it to Lord Mournloff so that he might take credit for resolving this crisis, I think he will reward you with any mead you choose. We should seek it. We should seize it!"

Shalm had finally decided that Jayn was beyond jesting. The fact that Jayn evidently understood – Shalm knew not how – the *significance* of the mead this night seemed even more extraordinary than the legend of the Silver Sieve. Perhaps Jayn *was* a sorceress! But if Shalm found her own mind to be unexpectedly translucent to Jayn, that did nothing about the opacity of Jayn herself.

"There is," Shalm said, "one mystery I must solve before I can move on this information. Why would you assist me? And don't tell me that it's just because you're 'bored,' because I will not believe you."

"You may believe me or not, as you choose," said Jayn, "but you have stated the simple truth of it. I *am* bored, and my boredom pulls me into many strange situations. But perhaps a bit of explanation will make this boredom more plausible to you. You see, every scrollmaster is assigned an area. One studies arms and armaments. Another, fell beasts. A third, fell magic. And so on. And finally myself. I was to become a master scribe of cobwebs. When I took my vows of poverty before the hallowed archives, I told myself that this was my brutal initiation. I was nineteen years old. Ten years later, I was still the master of cobwebs, and I told myself that I was 'paying my dues,' as they say. Someday I would get to study and scribe some deadly enchantment, some perilous geas, and so another fifteen years passed. Today, I have passed forty-four winters on this rock, and I have finally deduced that the scribelords simply do not like me. I was too talented and fierce to turn away entirely, so they gave me a job, and made me master of cobwebs, and master of cobwebs I have remained. And if this is not sufficient to explain my thirst for adventure, tonight or any night, then I judged you wrong. But I did not judge you wrong, did I?"

"Indeed, you did not," said Shalm. "I believe you. I want you to find adventure, and I want to find mead for myself. So we will work together in this. Where shall we go?"

"We shall go to the Burgomaster," Jayn said. "He despises both the magistrates and the Lich."

"Do you think he stole the Sieve?"

"I do not know, but it makes sense to ask him first."

"Then let us go at once!"

"No. First, let's enjoy our tea."

4

Shalm lifted her hand toward the heavy, hammered-bronze knocker on the great oak door.

"Wait!" hissed Jayn.

"What is it?" whispered Shalm.

"We should think of new names in case there are difficulties here. We don't want them to be able to find out who we really are."

Giddy with the warmth of the tea, the two had set forth from the hidden teahouse and added another thousand paces to their total. They passed through the Ruined District, kissed the Tavern District, passed swiftly through the Gold District, the University District, the Park District, the Theatre District, and finally entered the Sapphire District on the eastern shores of Firestone, where the sun would eventually rise.

This area was affluent compared to the rest of the beaten city, and while the houses were not ostentatious, candles still glowed in many full-glassed windows. While law required that the Nine Magistrates reside in their varied districts, most had a second home in the Sapphire District, and they flew its phthalo banners with pride. So did the most venerable judges, mages, scribes, emissaries, clerks, and functionaries. Not to mention the burgomaster. His stout house of stone and masonry flaunted its presence with flaming braziers that made shadows dance across his lawn, despite the lateness of the hour.

"Good idea," said Shalm. "What shall I name you?"

"I'd like to imagine that I am a member of the pickpocket's guild," said Jayn. "Name me Abstruel. Abstruel the Purloiner. Indeed, name me Abstruella Thineguard, Purloiner of Purses."

"Very good," said Shalm. "And you shall name me

Grana."

And with that, Shalm grasped the knocker and let it fall full upon the massive oaken door.

The women surveyed the quiet lawns and gardens about them and waited. The banners snapped in the dark night wind. The braziers threw their shadows. Leaves fell from their branches with a sigh before whispering down to the cobblestones. Shalm lifted the knocker to knock again, but then the door opened.

Before them stood a slightly confused-looking man with flushed pink skin, thick curls of tight red hair, and watchful dark eyes. He wore his robes of night and held a steaming clay mug of something alcoholic but, alas, it wasn't mead. The scent was too abrasive.

"It's quite late for you to be stopping by," the man said. "I already told your captain that I have no fear of rogues and ruffians. They have never turned upon my doorstep in fifteen years, and water poisoned or not, I don't imagine they will tonight."

"Burgomaster Florin!" said Shalm.

"Yes?" said the burgomaster.

"We bear tidings."

"Yes?"

"We are not the town guard."

"No? Then who are you?"

"You are looking upon Grana the Feared!" piped Jayn.

"Yes," said Shalm, warming to the role. "And this is Abstruella Thineguard, Purloiner of Purses."

"You are?" asked the burgomaster, becoming more confused by the minute.

"We are dangerous rogues," said Jayn.

"And miscreatinsh ruffians," said Shalm.

"Oh, dear!" wailed the burgomaster, and he started to shut the door again, but Shalm held her palm out and easily pushed the portal open. Jayn slipped around her friend and into the entrance, flanking the panicked burgomaster. She drew a silver letter opener from the folds of her robes. Shalm rattled her greatsword in its scabbard.

"Don't slay me!" yelped the burgomaster.

"Then do what we say," said Shalm.

"What do you want?"

"Mead."

Confusion crossed the burgomaster's face.

"But I haven't any mead!" he cried.

"Damn," said Shalm.

"In that case," said Jayn, "you can give us the Silver Sieve."

"The Sieve?" said the burgomaster.

"You know of it. The gifted artifact able to purify any

quantity of water? About such a size, or so I imagine."

And Jayn traced the shape of a large sieve with her letter opener.

"But I don't have that!"

"You hear that?" asked Jayn.

"It sounds suspicious to me," said Shalm. "First, you say you don't have mead, and then you say you don't have the Sieve. Next, you'll tell us that you don't have your robes of night."

"But obviously, I have my robes of night. I am wearing them!"

"Maybe we'll take those, then, since you don't have the Sieve or the mead. We could leave you shivering naked in front of your own house."

"And send you scurrying amidst the taverns!" grinned Jayn. "Another bright burnishing of your raptored reputation!"

"Please don't," said the burgomaster.

"Grana, will you please come inside and shut that door behind you?"

"With pleasure, Abruella."

Shalm stepped inside and shut the door.

"Let's sit and talk like reasonable ruffians," said Jayn. "Please tell me if you have tea, at least."

"Alas, I do not," said the burgomaster.

"Your prospects continue to dim by the moment."

The burgomaster reluctantly led his guests to a library, where they sat on a red floral chintz sofa. The burgomaster stood nervously before them, fiddling with his thumbs.

"I am aware of the Sieve's existence," said Jayn. "I am aware of its functionality. What I don't understand is why you haven't used it yet."

"I told you: I don't have it!" said the burgomaster. "If I had such a device, I would have used it weeks ago."

"You told us that the ensorceled river water was safe to drink. Town criers announced this in every district. But when you discovered that the water was contaminated, you knew that if anyone saw you using the Sieve, it would be an admission of the danger. You'd rather see the people of this town sicken and die than admit your fault in forcing us to drink that river water."

"I did not! I would not!"

"Or perhaps, you see in this some secret leverage you could use against the Nine Magistrates. They oppose your every design. You must believe you can bring them to heel with promises to heal the water. Or that they will be pilloried in their corners before you ever taste an injury for your heinous misdeeds!"

"I do not!"

"I think it's simpler than that," said Shalm. "I don't think that Burgomaster Florin poisoned the water, nor do I believe that he has the power to heal it. No, he is in a mess of his own making and is twisting and turning to find his way out. Yet he cannot."

"Indeed, I am afraid you are correct, ruffian Grana. I have no power. I am a victim in this as much as you are!"

"But he's the burgomaster!" protested Jayn. "The most powerful man in Firestone!"

"No," said Shalm. "You were right. I was wrong. Because the Lich must have deputies here in Firestone. They must be far more powerful than any magistrate or burgomaster."

"You say 'more powerful,'" said Florin with some bitterness. "The fact of the matter is that I have no power whatsoever. You have heard, perhaps, of Overlord Margate, the servant of the Lich? When Margate first arrived from the Bittle Citadel, he bore a scroll from the Lich stating that he was to take charge of Firestone. Since then, the magistrates and I have had to set aside our hatred for each other and follow Margate's commands."

As he spoke, Florin glanced nervously at an ornate portrait that hung over his fireplace. Shalm stood and crossed the room to examine the piece. It was a realistic painting of a corpse, half-skeleton and half-rotting flesh. The skeleton held his right hand up, his thumb out, fingers together like a mitten. It made the shape of the realm, this realm of Lichigan, and the Lich pointed to the location of Firestone on the palm of this bony map. Two twin stars glittered cruelly from the depths of his eye sockets, and he was dressed in moldering finery. Purple and green. Shalm got the unsettling feeling that the unholy creature was watching her. A small gold plate beneath the painting read:

𝔄 gift to 𝔅urgomaster 𝔉lorin
𝔉rom his friend Cannos the 𝔏ich
𝔍n thanks for faithful service
𝔗o the people of 𝔉irestone.

"If there is a Sieve," said the burgomaster, "then Overlord Margate must have it. All artifacts and treasures of the city were turned over to his care when he took command. If you want, you can ask him for it, but he is not as harmless as I am. He is deadly! Do not tell him that it was I who told you all this."

"Where can you find him?"

"He resides in the Mournloff Mausoleum in the Bones District. He is perilous at any hour and especially at night!"

"Let's go, Grana."

Burgomaster Florin breathed an audible sigh of relief as Jayn left the room. But Shalm paused in the entryway and regarded the burgomaster with a stern, slightly sad expression.

"Why did you drink the water when they said it was dangerous?" she asked. "Why did you say it was safe?"

"I wanted my power back," said Florin, with a stubbornly burgeoning pride. "If the Lich and his servants were ever going to return this city to my control, I had to do what they said. I didn't have a choice!"

"You were mistaken," said Shalm. "You didn't get your power from the Lich. You got it from the people of Firestone, who chose you to be their burgomaster. And you could have told the truth about the water. You could have learned and shared what you learned. You were trusted. Trust is a kind of power."

The burgomaster rose to his feet, grasping at Shalm as if at a glittering treasure. But Shalm turned her back and left the room, leaving Burgomaster Florin with his many guttering candles.

5

Shalm reluctantly admitted an error of a dozen steps plus or minus her official count of 4,100 by the time they reached the Bone District. The consequences thereof were something she didn't want to contemplate, so she redoubled her efforts. It wasn't easy. The fog lay thick here, and the cracks split the cobbles. Plus, with Jayn's incessant chatter and Shalm's own troubled thoughts, she found it very hard to keep count. The numbers chased the thoughts, and the thoughts chased the numbers, and neither could drive the other fully from her brain.

The Bones District lay far in the west of Firestone, where the sun sets and dies each day. There, they found a wrought-iron gate with splintery spears barring their way. An arcane lock fastened the heavy gate.

"I don't suppose you've got a bit of wire?" Jayn asked. "I've had some practice at picking these ..."

As the scrollmaster fumbled about her robes, Shalm caught Jayn about the waist, lifted her high overhead, and threw her bodily over the spiky bars. Then Shalm caught two of the spears near their points and heaved herself over and into the cemetery. Jayn got to her feet and brushed the dirt off of her knees.

"Much faster," she said. "And more efficient, too. Just warn me next time."

Shalm grunted in answer. The wind roared, the fog split, the branches tumbled, and freed acorns rattled their way to earth. Jayn lit a small candle, shielding its timid flame against the breeze, and the two made their way into the thicket of gravestones. This district was extensive, and despite the blindness of the dark, they could hear the wind wailing against the sculptures and mausoleums. Hills and towering oak trees rose all around. Eventually, the sharp-toothed fence and the fumes of the city vanished behind them. Now, all was thin mist, cool air, and graves.

Shalm shivered. They hadn't asked Burgomaster Florin precisely what Overlord Margate *was*, but if he was spending his nights in this cemetery, he must be sorcery-bound in some way. Shalm had visited the Bones District before. It was lovely with its golden, overhanging branches and the river turning through it, but everyone knew not to come here at night. Here dwelt noxious creatures far more deadly than the bugbears of the

Ruined District. UnDead things. They could freeze your blood in your arteries, or steal the motion from your limbs, or feed upon your living flesh. Some of them could only be killed with silver. Shalm wondered if Jayn's letter opener was made out of silver. Shalm's sword certainly wasn't. Her dagger wasn't, either, though its many other powers were slow to reveal themselves. She drew her dagger and held it tight in her fist.

"There!" said Jayn.

Her candle flickered against the dark, and Shalm could just make out the contours of a large mausoleum. Its gray stone thrust like a mountain from the earth, and black bars covered its dark stained windows. The name 'MOURNLOFF' had been deeply incised above the entrance. The heavy stone door stood ajar.

Jayn approached the door and thrust her head and candle inside the dark space.

"Overlord Margate?"

Her voice echoed about the cavernous interior.

Her head reemerged.

"Nobody's home," she said, but Shalm's ears caught a faint *whirring* sound, followed by a clean, crisp click. She reached out and yanked Jayn back from the portal. Three small darts flighted out of the darkness, struck the door, and fell.

"That was a close thing," said Jayn, brushing herself off. "Thank you, Shalm. It appears I owe you a debt. What was that?"

Shalm knelt and picked up one of the darts. She waved it under her nose and breathed in its acidic stench, touched the tip to her tongue, then spit roughly.

"Is it deadly?" asked Jayn.

"It's paralyzing. If I hadn't pulled you back, I'd have been carrying you out of here."

"I'm lucky I've got you here with me."

"This trap wasn't part of the tomb. It's been arranged recently. This poison is fresh."

"Do you think it was set by the person who left the door open?"

"It signifies."

In the distance, a fallen branch cracked, followed by a low male voice swearing.

"Quickly!" hissed Jayn, darting to the side behind an obelisk.

Shalm knelt behind a cairn. She held her dagger and her breath, listening.

6

First came the eyes. Dull red were they, like the embers of a long-resting fire, and they soundlessly advanced upon the vault. Shalm recalled Jayn's words from the beginning of the night: "he has very powerful deputies here, and they live here, and they gaze down on these streets with their red-glowing eyes, but they never come out during the day."

The eyes arrived at the open door. Shalm peeked over the bank of stones to get a better view and discerned a black-cloaked figure kneeling. He had picked up one of the fallen darts and rolled it between his fingers. He stood and turned.

"Who's there?" the figure asked.

Shalm stepped out from behind the cairn, her dagger menacing. The dark figure chuckled.

"Do you think that can injure me?" he said.

"Hasn't failed me yet," Shalm said.

The figure advanced upon her. She could see him better now. Black trousers and a black tunic. A black cloak rippling in the breeze behind him. A fine black hat sporting a rotting red feather. And white hair and a white beard. A bloodless face, striated with red wrinkles. Those burning eyes …

"This can injure you," chirped Jayn as she stepped out from behind the obelisk. She held the letter cutter out before her.

The figure rounded upon her.

"Are you sure?"

"Blade of silver, grip of cold iron, and I've enchanted it besides. I'm not sure, but are you really wanting to take chances? All I'm risking is my mortal skin, but an immortal like you? I mean, you'd be risking everything!"

The figure stopped his advance. He chuckled again, but resignation had replaced the menace. He returned to the open crypt door and palmed the poisoned darts. He hid them in an inner pocket.

"Poison of mandrake and baneberry. Easy to procure, difficult to distill. Still, it kept you out of my tomb."

"Out of the Mournloff Tomb, you mean!"

"Maybe he is a Mournloff, brought back from death with chthonic sorcery!" said Shalm.

"No," said Jayn. "This is the vampire Margate, sent here by the Lich to serve as his overlord. We are honored to meet you, Overlord Margate."

The figure's smile was strained.

"The honor is all mine," he said. "Though I am not acquainted with you from before. What are your names? And who told you where I reside?"

"We need your consultation," said Jayn, plowing ahead as if he hadn't spoken. "We seek the Silver Sieve. We have reason to believe that it is in your possession."

Margate sighed.

"I wish that it was in my possession," he said. "It would have been of great use these last few weeks.

"Then you confirm its existence."

"I confirm nothing. It would be reckless of me to do so. But I begin to discern traces of your vocation. You seek to trap me with words, in a web of my own weaving. You have spent time among the scrolls, young one!"

"Not so young …" Jayn said, with both her voice and weapon trembling.

"All are young to me."

Shalm put her hand on the hilt of her sword.

"Is it true you are his deputy?" she asked. "The Lich?"

"She would know," Margate said with a nod toward Jayn. "This was all become official in the chambers of the Bittle Citadel, scribed in the blood of virgins, and made known among the 83 counts. Peasants and wastrels know little of it, which explains, I suppose, your ignorance, but those with discernment know what came to pass."

"Why?" asked Shalm. "We have a burgomaster and magistrates."

"Firestone has become thin since your carriage makers left. The Lich of Lichigan requires tithe. Firestone did not pay. Your magistrates told us that you *could* not pay. But the Lich assured them that you could. His decree put me above them all – your tiny magistrates, your trivial burgomaster – and I promised him that Firestone would render up all that had been asked. And it has."

"We have always paid tithe to the Citadel!" said Jayn. "But

in days before the Lich took up the crown, the Citadel has returned some of those funds for us to use as we need. To repair and guard the walls. To care for widows and orphans. To drain the swamps where fever breeds. To draw clean water from clear cisterns. But since Cannos ascended, none of this has come to pass. The Citadel takes what it wishes but renders nothing back in exchange."

As Jayn said the name 'Cannos,' Margate's fiery eyes glanced nervously toward the door to the tomb, but he quickly recovered his composure.

"You ought not to name him. Best to simply call him 'the Lich.'" he admonished.

"It must seem like a waste," said Jayn. "You delivered the riches of this city into his palm, but he has confined you to a tomb in a thicket of wild!"

Margate ignored these taunts. Once again, he fixed his eyes on Shalm, who regarded him with sincerity, perplexity, even sadness. His curse had blessed him with vision in the dark, and as he studied her face, he saw in her eyes deep wells, cool and liquid, a tremor, a disquiet, that all of the UnDead knew only too well. This breathing thing knew deep pain.

Shalm similarly studied Margate's eyes, and as she looked into their dull, red, pupilless skim of a surface, like molten glass, she felt an overwhelming sense of weariness overtake her. She could have rested before that hearth. She could have forsaken her quest for mead, her count of the steps she had taken, and all of the other necessary measures that absorbed her attention, constantly, relentlessly, for hours each day, essential tasks, mandatory rituals, and memories, and guilts, and rested before that warm hearth, had she not known that Jayn stood nearby, watching and guarding.

"Why did you do it?"

Shalm heard her own voice, and it reminded her of the coarseness of burlap, of stinging nettles, of the braying of a donkey, of everything rude and cold of Margate's red eyes, the comfort of the earth, its burning core.

"What did I do that I should wonder at my reason?" said the one with the eyes.

"You told us to take our water from the river. Nobody wanted to. We told you it was poison. The Lich's sorcerers told us that it was clean. They were wrong. They deceived us. They are fiends."

Margate's voice came deep, like the hum of some distant engine.

"The chthonic sorcery that we use to cleanse the water is twisted and mysterious. Few fully understand it. I discerned the expense you all paid to have water ensorceled by the Dire Straits. I wanted to free you to tithe the Citadel as it asked. I wanted to free you from the mandate of the Lich. I wanted to free you from myself. I wanted to free you."

Shalm felt the world's weariness flowing through her, but this voice told her that that was all a burden she could lay down.

Maybe she should simply sheathe her knife and curl up near one of these tombstones. The dried leaves and withered branches would keep her warm until the dawning sun.

"You speak lies, ageless one, even if you speak them in pleasant tones," said Jayn. Her voice cut through Shalm's torpor, and she tightened her grip on the dagger. "You were right that I have read many scrolls about you and your master. Now let me tell you what I have read. The river water was a temporary measure to remove Firestone from the sorcerers of Dire Straits. You meant to dig new cisterns that would employ new sorcerers and wizards and ... well diggers! They would pay the burgomaster and yourself for this contract. You planned to pay out the Lich's tithe with your right hand and to enrich yourself with the left."

"There is little hidden truth in the whisperings of fishwives and chambermaids!" snarled Margate.

"Ah, but there is much truth in the inkings of the scrollmasters of Firestone!"

"Then you claim your identity and reveal yourself."

"I confirm nothing. It would be reckless of me to do so."

"You have many words," said Margate. "But your companion has discernment."

He turned his gaze back toward Shalm, but the spell had been broken. Now she watched him warily, the small dagger gleaming between them.

41

"The law of the Lich is the law," said Margate.

"It matters not, liar," said Jayn. "We seek the Sieve."

"Where shall we find it?" asked Shalm.

"I told you that I do not possess it!" said Margate.

"It isn't in the treasury," said Jayn.

"It isn't with the burgomaster or the magistrates," said Shalm.

"Where did Cannos bid you hide it?" asked Jayn.

Again, Margate's eyes flicked toward the open door to the Mournloff tomb.

"I see!" cried Jayn. "It is one of his most valuable possessions here, so he bid you hide it in your resting place!"

"That is quite absurd," said Margate. "We would never put such a treasure in a tomb!"

But as he spoke, Jayn moved toward the mausoleum and ducked in through the open door. Margate started to follow, but Shalm cut him off, holding the dagger before him.

"Why don't you draw your sword?" he asked.

"The sword is to scare," Shalm said. "The dagger drinks blood."

Margate hesitated.

"By the Gods ..." Jayn's voice echoed through the open door. "Grana, you're not going to believe this!"

"What is it, uh, Abstruella? Is it a Sieve?"

"No! It is not, alas!"

"Is it a flagon of mead?"

"Unfortunately, 'tis not."

"Then what?"

"A portrait. We saw its copy earlier tonight. Listen to the inscription: 'A Gift to Overlord Margate from His friend Cannos the Lich, In thanks for faithful service to the Bittle Citadel!"

"Stop naming him!" hissed Margate.

"Is it a portrait of the Lich?" called out Shalm.

"'Tis!" answered Jayn.

Margate advanced a foot.

Shalm retreated a foot. She was half inside the tomb now. Margate grinned, and Shalm spied two fangs, wicked and serrated. He took another step. She retreated a step. She was inside the tomb now, and Margate's form filled the doorway, a ghastly silhouette illuminated only by the baleful light of those twin red lights.

"Jayn!" called out Shalm.

"Yes?"

"I think he intends to trap us in here."

"We'll have to drive him back. We're living. He's not. We need air."

And then Jayn was at Shalm's side, brandishing her letter opener. Margate's arms were on the mausoleum door. He was starting to press it closed. For the first time that evening, Shalm pulled her greatsword from its scabbard, wielding it in her left hand as her right held the dagger. They pressed through the door, blades extended, the sword flashing side to side, kicking up sparks as it struck against the metal hinges. Margate retreated before this onslaught, and as they reemerged into the night again, Jayn was surprised to see dried blood covering the length of Shalm's sword. Then she realized that she saw not blood, but rust, thick across the once-tempered surface, marring its sharpness and beauty.

But Margate moved fast. He flowed, more than ran, in a semicircle, cutting away toward a hillock rising to his right, drawing Shalm and Jayn after him. He darted from the shadows, now wielding a sword of his own, and the clang of metal against metal grated against the night. Shalm's sword had stopped Margate's blade from parting Jayn's head from her body.

"Again, I am in your service!" panted Jayn.

"And I am but paying you back," answered Shalm, parrying back a volley of blows. "He almost had me hypnotized earlier, but you shattered his enchantment."

"We had best stay together!" said Jayn, aiming a cut at Margate's leg, forcing his attention away from Shalm for a moment.

Then Jayn and Shalm were on the offense again, pushing

Margate farther up the hill into the trees that crowded its crown, and his sword flew to and fro as he blocked the three blades that cut against him again and again. Together, the two women seemed a match for the vampire, though just barely, but Shalm already recognized the deception in this advantage: they, as mortals, must tire with combat, and quickly. Margate could fight breathlessly until the sun rose.

"We'd better best this foe quickly, Abruella!" she shouted.

"I had the same thought, Grana!" answered Jayn.

They entered a clearing at the top of the hill. The blades sang, parting the damp air, and the fog that gathered in the shadows glowed phosphorescent as though fairies had alighted to cheer on the sport and chant for the blood they hoped to see soon spilled.

"My friend, you told me that you sought adventure," said Shalm. "Is this the adventure you sought?"

"If we make it out alive, I am full of mirth," said Jayn. "But if I die, I'll never forgive you."

Round they went, almost flanking Margate, but he was light on his toes, and once or twice, some dagger or sword seemed to make contact with the vampire, but his skin parted as if made of mist only to flow together, intact, when the blow had completed its course. But now, Jayn overextended herself on an attack, and Margate slid to the ground on one knee, bringing his sword up and lodging it in Jayn's shoulder. She swore, and the blood spurted out. Shalm lunged and impaled him from behind, but there was no blood in his UnDead body. She pulled her rusted sword back just in time to repel the counterattack.

Now, seeing Jayn's wound and Shalm's tiredness, the vampire drove forward again, pushing them back down the opposite side of the hill and into the cemetery beyond. They moved by sense, their feet anticipating twisted roots, obscured holes, and tussocks, dancing as they went, their blades kissing, the cemetery quiet as all its creatures silenced themselves to witness this mighty battle.

Then Margate looked at Shalm and spoke gibberish.

He glanced at Jayn and spoke nonsense.

"He's casting a spell!" cried Jayn.

Margate held his right hand skyward and pointed his claws to the sky while thrusting his blade into the earth on the left. He called out a single fell syllable. A shudder went out from Margate, roiling the gravestones, trembling the turf. Shalm and Jayn sensed, more than they saw, the movement of bodies buried all too shallow in the loamy soil. The ground beneath each marker seemed to heave in protest. And again, Margate swung his mighty blade.

"Abru – Abru – where did you put your candle?" gasped Shalm.

"I left it in the tomb."

"Is it still lit?"

"I think so."

"Can you hold him off for a moment?"

"I can try!"

Jayn hadn't even stopped speaking when Shalm broke away from the combat, running in a broad arc back around the base of the hill. She squinted through the dark at the mausoleums and finally found what she sought. A dark lantern hung from a stone shepherd's crook mounted beside a mossy door. But a root wrapped around her ankle, and Shalm sprawled on her face. Her sword went flying from her grasp. The root twisted and dug woody nails into her flesh. She kicked at it. The root let go. It splayed fingers. Five, glistening and rotting. It wasn't a root at all but a hand thrust from the damp earth. Shalm struck with her dagger and severed three of its fingers. The hand continued to twitch in her direction. Shalm stumbled to her feet, retrieved her sword and lantern, and continued her circuit of the hill.

Two dark figures rose up, one skeletal and the other bloated with the gasses of decomposition. Shalm decapitated the latter. As its head went flying, she buried her sword in its belly with three quick thrusts, and a black, viscous liquid poured from the wounds. A fifth blow lopped its legs out from beneath it. Skeletal fingers clasped the back of Shalm's neck. She reached back and wrapped her fingers around the skeleton's mossy ribcage. She flung the UnDead creature over her head and against a tree. With a splintering sound, the bones broke and fell to the earth. Again. Shalm raced. Jayn wasn't a match for Margate alone, and every second she took increased the chances that Shalm would return only to find her companion dead.

47

Could he possess her, too? Shalm wondered.

She made it to the Mournloff mausoleum and hurtled inside. Sure enough, by candlelight, she made out the painted visage of the Lich glaring hatefully at her. *I hate you too,* thought Shalm, but there wasn't any time. She lifted the painting from its mount and strapped it upon her back like a quiver of arrows. She snatched up the candle and hurried back outside, awkwardly shielding the feeble fire against the wind while balancing her two blades and the lantern in her other arm. Shalm found three more zombies waiting for her, but they were clumsily shedding pieces of themselves as they went. She easily maneuvered around them, kicking the leader into his companions, and hurried back up the hill and down the other side.

To have said that Shalm arrived just at the last instant could have almost been an understatement. Hard-pressed, Jayn was falling back before Margate's fearsome while also ducking and twisting around three zombies who groped and clawed at her face. It was amazing to Shalm that the scrollmaster hadn't fallen already.

"Overlord Margate!" Shalm called from the brow of the hill.

Down below, the attack continued, though Margate looked up toward Shalm.

"We have not injured you yet, but we might."

Shalm dropped the portrait of the Lich into the soil and poured lantern oil all over it. She held the dripping candle over the mess at her feet.

"Pause," said Margate.

The zombies relented.

Jayn reached out and cut off a rotting hand from pure spite.

"Well?" asked Margate.

"As I said, we have not injured you. We walk free."

Jayn nudged the zombies aside and scrambled up the hill to stand beside Shalm.

"By Cannos, is that all?" asked Margate.

"Where is the Sieve?" asked Shalm.

Margate grinned again.

"It is where you can never retrieve it. When I took over Firestone, I sold most of its treasures. I sold your Sieve to a Demon of the Roots of the World. Its lair resides beneath the now-corrupted sewers drawing water from the Firestone River. You will find the entrance where seven willows grow over seven graves. But you will not be able to open it. It can be unsealed only from the living dream of a repentant murderer who has sipped of the Ichor of Muin Ellim."

"Thank you," said Shalm. "We never needed to battle at all. You could have told us that when we first met you."

"You are alone in the heart of my domain," Margate intoned. "What makes you think you will survive to see the sunrise?"

"I've learned not to look into your eyes. Now you will search for mine in vain. We will flee. You will not pursue us. You'll be too busy putting out this fire."

With a quick grace, Shalm knelt and set the portrait aflame.

Then she stood and ran, and Jayn ran beside her.

They ran in the dark, they ran in the wind, they ran from the vampire and all of his zombies, but above all, they ran from the malicious, detestable screams that flew from the lips of the painted Lich!

7

Once Shalm and Jayn had cleared the cemetery gates again, they stood, hunched over, hands on knees, drinking in the damp night air.

"The portrait screamed," panted Shalm.

"The Lich," gasped Jayn. "The painting must be a –"

"Hold fast!" cried a voice from the dark.

Shalm looked up and saw the surrounding shadows take shape and confirm. *More of the UnDead?* No, these were figures of flesh and blood. Brass buckles clicked against the metal studs of leather armor. Iron clasps on leather caps. The Firestone Town

Guard. There were five of them surrounding Shalm and Jayn.

"What is this?" Shalm asked.

"A magistrate lit a beacon," said the captain. "She saw the two of you entering the Bones District."

"We were out for a midnight stroll," quipped Shalm.

"You were tangling with Overlord Margate, and now the magistrates will have you for tortures and interrogations."

Jayn drew her letter opener again.

Shalm drew her sword almost languorously.

"Please, don't make us kill you," she said.

"Our bows are trained. Sheathe your weapon."

As he spoke, Shalm started her advance. Then a crossbow snapped, but Shalm had already flung herself backward, belly upward, feet and palms anchored, while the keen bolt flew just above her. Shalm converted her momentum into a roll and sprang to her feet inches from another guardsman, who staggered as he tried to draw his weapon. She drove the hilt of her sword into his face, pushed into rotation, and swung the blade into the side of another guard. The rusted blade didn't break the leather armor, but the guard's grunt confirmed that Shalm had staggered her. Shalm brought her dagger hilt down on the woman's head and felled her to the earth. Meanwhile, the first guard reeled and yelled, blinded by his own blood. Already, the odds looked friendlier.

Jayn had sprung into action beside Shalm. She'd flung her

letter opener into a guard's foot, and as he frantically pulled at the slender blade, she leapfrogged over his back, drawing his short sword as she went. The guards' ambush had already gone terribly awry, and now it was four on two, with two of the four wounded.

"The magistrate sent you?" asked Jayn. "Or was it the Lich?"

One of the guards looked at the captain in surprise.

The captain gave a quick shake of her head.

"We were going to leave off with fingernails and toenails," she said. "After this, it'll be the rack for you both."

Shalm sighed.

"They're idiots," she told Jayn. "If we don't flee them, we'll have to kill them all."

"I want to slay villains," said Jayn. "Not foolish guardlings. Let's hoof."

8

Shalm and Jayn quickly outpaced the scattered guards but kept running for many minutes, following the thickets of poplars and maples down to the gurgling river. They finally stopped to find their wind in a gentle copse on the margin of the City of the Stars District. Looking upstream, they could discern the mazy alleys of the Tavern District and the marble-columned towers of the Gold District beyond. The last guttering torches went out, one by one. It was late now. Far past midnight. A desolate hour when the streets of Firestone had emptied utterly.

Jayn daubed at the wound on her shoulder and produced unguent and bandages from a hidden pocket deep in her robes. She gritted her teeth as she treated the cut.

"'Tisn't much of an injury, truly," she said.

Shalm sighed. She felt sore from all of her exertions. Worse, she had lost track of the number of steps she had taken. Utterly lost track. She was ignorant. And still meadless.

"What's wrong?" asked Jayn.

"Nothing," said Shalm. "We've escaped. We've escaped twice. How many times are we going to dare luck to defeat us."

"Probably at least a *couple* more times. It's still hours 'til dawn."

"The guards said they been sent by one of the Nine Magistrates. What is their quarrel with us?"

"The magistrates must know that Overlord Margate resides in the Bones District. They figured it was one of their fellow magistrates plotting against them."

Shalm snorted in disgust. "Can they truly be preoccupied with their jealousies right now? Their city is bleeding. Their people are poisoned."

"Never underestimate the jealousies and pettiness of the

magistrates."

Jayn pondered Shalm.

"You don't look like the trusting type," she went on. "You look much more fearsome than me. But I think that you are too trusting, and I believe that you are a newcomer to Firestone."

"True, and true," said Shalm.

"In time, you will understand. In time, nothing that happens here will surprise you anymore. It won't take long."

"Indeed, I'm becoming less surprised by the hour. Ever since I met you, I've been making enemies of dangerous people."

"Did you find the burgomaster dangerous? He said that he was powerless. Were you ever afraid of those absurd guards?"

"The overlord was powerful ..."

"I'll not challenge that."

"It cost you your weapon. A blade of silver and a grip of cold iron? That was a valuable instrument to have lost!"

"It was an ordinary letter opener. I lied to force his distance."

"It was a good lie."

"What about your blades? That rusted sword? That curved knife?"

"I trust the sword; it will not kill. I mistrust the dagger; it will. I try to keep my hands on both."

They had rested long enough that their breath had finally settled into a regular rhythm. The river murmured as it rolled out of the city behind them. A single, living cricket creaked somewhere out in the weeds. The night felt cool and still. It was a pleasant night, and for a moment, Shalm wished that she could forget and walk away from all the clash and havoc. And yet ...

"Still no mead," she said.

"We're close, you know," said Jayn.

"Close to what?"

"To retrieving the Sieve."

"It's been claimed by a demon!"

"You have been quite handy in combat," said Jayn. "And I think I've also acquitted myself well. We could best it, I think! We would be heroes of the city! And you could get your mead, and maybe I could finally get the recognition I've so long deserved. Do you know what spells the scrollmasters can make if I bring them the head of a Demon of the Roots of the World?!"

"It doesn't matter. We have to open the gate in the sewers. That's what Margate said. We don't have what we need to do that."

"Yes," said Jayn. "We're only missing one thing."

"The Ichor of Muin Ellim," said Shalm.

"A repentant murderer," said Jayn at the same time.

The two regarded each other for a long, quiet moment

55

before Jayn finally spoke.

"I have the ichor," said Jayn. "I bought it from a peddler years ago. I can brew it as a tea. It does bring waking dreams."

She spoke guardedly, as one fearful of what she was about to hear.

"And I am a repentant murderer," said Shalm, quietly, as one who is fearful of what she had said.

9

Having exchanged their secrets, Shalm and Jayn set out wordlessly on the final stage of their mission. So focused were they upon their quest that they did not notice an ungainly shadow step out from behind a beech tree and creep along after them.

Jayn led Shalm across the footbridge, and many long tracks beyond, to her house tucked in the silent cowls of the City of the Moon District. This district, larger and more populous than any other in the city, was also the most neglected. Many of its houses had become hovels, its cottages calamities, its tenements terrible. Jayn's own house was quite small: a sitting room that doubled as a bedroom, a cook room with an enclosed cistern, and a tiny courtyard with an outhouse. A dusty dirt track sinewed like a serpent toward the front door. Jayn and Shalm followed this path and went inside. The soft light of an oil lantern illuminated the windows of the front room. The following shadow waited out in the street.

Inside, Jayn warmed her hands by the small flame and studied Shalm. Shalm's expression was unreadable. No emotion, joyful or angry or fearful or remorseful, crossed her. But the flickering flame made her face into a skull, and her deep-set eyes resembled empty sockets. Involuntarily, the scrollmaster wondered if Shalm's crime and her thirst for mead, her constant counting, were connected.

"I would not have guessed that you were a murderer," Jayn said.

"Plenty are," hedged Shalm.

"You will not tell me what happened?"

"I will not."

"Alas, the scroll yields its secrets only when the author chooses. Yet I deduce that you are more than a hay-baler."

"Plenty are," Shalm repeated.

"I cannot make you trust me. Your mistrust must come of a reason. But I can ask you to let me help you. If you are not repentant, then you will not be able to open the gate."

Shalm laughed sadly.

"But one span ago, you mocked me for being too trusting, Jayn. Now I see that your cynicism has misled you. Most murderers are repentant. For what can be less forgiven than a murder? Only the murdered can forgive, and they are gone forever."

"I believe you. Let me brew the tea."

The ichor was a rare substance extracted from the blood of the horned worms of Muin Ellim, which lived in the desert lands far to the south of Lichigan. When concentrated and dried, this blood became a resin. By adding boiling water, one could consume this ichor. But the worms were bewitched animals. They burrowed deep beneath the earth. Therefore, the spells weaved were chthonic and full of deception.

As Jayn poured the water into the mug, a pungent odor, like wet dirt and rotting wood, filled the room.

"Does it taste as it smells?" asked Shalm.

"It tastes much worse," said Jayn.

"Why did you buy it?"

"Scrollwork is obscure and fatiguing. Sometimes your knowledge fails. You need to stir your dreams for answers. I have many substances stronger than this. I drink tea at all times, and not always for pleasure. But now you must drink."

Shalm lifted the mug to her lips. The tea was bitter – bitter beyond belief – and her whole self convulsed with the desire to expel it from her body.

"Hold it down," said Jayn.

Shalm clenched her teeth and held.

"Drink again," Jayn said.

Shalm drank.

"And again," said Jayn.

Shalm drank until the small clay mug was empty.

"Can I have some water now?" asked Shalm.

Wordlessly, Jayn went to the cistern and filled the mug with water. Shalm drank it.

"What now?" she asked.

"The ichor is within you. Soon it will start showing you visions. But they will not do us any good here. No. Now we must leave. We must go to the entrance to the ancient sewers, where seven willows grow over seven graves."

"Do you know this place?"

"I know many of the secret places scattered about Firestone. This, we will find in the Anglers District, near the old graveyard, just inside the city walls. It is not far from here."

"Then let's go. Let's finish this task. Let's get the Sieve. Let's get this damned night over with. Although it's getting harder and harder for me to see how this will get me any mead!"

When Jayn emerged into the starless night again, she clutched the small lantern and carried a stout club, a poor exchange for the lost letter opener. Shalm followed, eyes darting with the visions already. They weren't seen things. They were voices out of her past. Voices of those she had wronged. They called out to her sadly, and Shalm sought their faces but could not find them. The two women slipped into the street and departed north toward the city walls, and the shadow followed. Three travelers moving from dark to dark, but no darkness as large as what they carried inside.

10

With Shalm entranced by the early visions, Jayn took the lead, ready to bargain with or brain any interlopers barring their way. Even during the day, the City of the Moon was known to be treacherous, and daylight was still far away. And yet the streets were utterly empty, as though a spirit of warning had settled upon Firestone.

Now they came at last to the city walls, mossy and unattended this far north, and at their stony feet, a small circle of gravestones overhung by massive willows.

"Are we here?" asked Shalm.

Her voice sounded strange and hollow like she was calling out from the bottom of a well.

"We are," said Jayn. "How are the visions? Not too terrible, I hope?"

"They *are* terrible. But I don't know why you call them visions. I hear voices, but I don't see a thing."

"Strange. For me, they were always visions. Come with me."

Jayn led them to the center of the small grove, got down on her knees, and started feeling around through the grass.

"Here we are!" she said. "It's almost entirely overgrown."

And Jayn pulled a thick mat of sod away from a large iron disc set in the ground. In the middle of it, a large iron ring.

"Ordinarily, we would just pull this up," Jayn said. "I'm not strong enough myself, but I suspect –"

Shalm spun on her heel, drawing her dagger, and whipped the blade into the gloom. There was a small shriek of surprise from the darkness. Shalm had drawn her sword and rushed into the darkness before Jayn had even gotten to her feet. She waited, listening to a sound of pleading, then by a great blow, then a heaving voice, male, trying to recover its breath. Then Shalm reappeared with Burgomaster Florin slung over her shoulders like he might have been a sack of onions. She tossed him down before Jayn.

"We've been attacked by just about everybody tonight!" snapped Shalm. "Were you about to have a run at us as well, then? You're more cunning than the town guard but much less than Margate, and we survived him, too!"

"Please! Please!" begged Florin. "I mean no harm! I was coming to help you!"

"Help at this unlit hour?" asked Jayn. "Help unasked? Help when every sound has become an ambush? What makes you think we wish such help, burgomaster?!"

She brandished her club, then let it fall to her side, realizing that Shalm was far more intimidating.

"Answer her!" snapped Shalm.

"Well, it's this. I know that you survived Margate. I didn't expect you to go to meet him. And then you did. Then, my bell rang. We each have a little bell – me and the magistrates – and it rings for us whenever any of us has summoned the town guard. A simple spell. I heard it, and I knew it must be about you. So I hurried out to the Bones District, and I saw you fighting the guard. I knew then that you had survived the vampire and his allies. I heard the scream and realized that you had defied the Lich himself. And you survived! You must be cunning rogues! Or mighty warriors! Or deadly sorcerers! Mercy, oh mercy!"

The woman with the rusted sword and the scrollmaster with the giant robes exchanged glances and tried not to laugh.

"And you thought that maybe you could succeed where others have failed?" asked Shalm.

"No, no, no, I want you to succeed! I want you to win the Silver Sieve! I wanted to see if you were serious."

"We are serious. We have come to the entrance of the ruin where it is hidden, according to Margate. Do you believe us?"

"Yes! Yes!"

"Do you want to fetch it yourself?"

"No! No! It's terrible down there. Terrible!"

"Then you'd better let us retrieve it."

"Yes, please do, please bring it back! Only bring it to me!"

"There it is," said Jayn. "There's his angle."

"If I have the Sieve, I can restore clean water to the whole city of Firestone. I could even defy the Lich. You said I had the power that came from the people of this city. Return me the Sieve, and I can use that power for the good of all!"

"We were going to give it to Mournloff," said Jayn.

"No, no, don't do that! He's in league with the Lich. They'll keep it for themselves or sell it back to us at a price we cannot hope to pay! Give it to me when you return!"

"What about my friend's mead?"

"*I* could ask Mournloff for some mead. He'd turn you away from his gates, but from me, the request would be a mere favor."

"Allow me a few words with my colleague, Florin."

"Yes, yes, of course," stammered the hapless burgomaster, retreating just out of the circle of trees and making a show of putting his fingers in her ears.

"Was that really him talking that whole time?" asked Shalm as soon as Florin had stepped away.

"Yes," said Jayn. "He said a lot."

"Better than the other voices I'm hearing."

"Florin says that Mournloff is in league with the Lich," Jayn went on. "It would make sense. The Mournloffs are an old family, and very rich, very powerful. They want to control everything in Firestone because it's the city they have helped rule for a century. It would make sense for them to form an alliance with the Lich. Remember, Margate is overlord, but he was staying in the Mournloff tomb."

"So what do you say?" asked Shalm.

"I say we take Florin up on his offer ... for now. We can always change our mind once we have the Sieve, if we think there's something better to do with it. But at the least it would mean we're not making another enemy tonight."

"I agree with this plan," said Shalm. "But let's talk for another several minutes to keep him in doubt."

"How many steps have we taken tonight?"

"I don't know. I lost track after our battle with the guards."

"Maybe you should count stars, instead." Jayn gestured toward the cloudy sky.

"I have been. I've counted nine. There were breaks in the clouds twice. Four stars, and then five."

"Impressive. I haven't seen a single star tonight."

"Burgomaster!" cried Shalm. "Return!"

Florin returned to the clearing, looking worried.

"We agree to your proposal," said Jayn. "But we have conditions."

"Perhaps you want to bargain after you've retrieved the Sieve?" said Florin.

"No, we'll bargain now. First, we don't want the guards giving us any more trouble tonight, so if that bell of yours sounds again, we want *you* to be the one to greet them, and explain the trouble away, and send them back home."

"Understood."

"Second, if we get the Sieve, I want you to use all your influence and all your connections to promote more scrolllords within Firestone. The libraries are too empty these days, and it fills the masters' heads with cobwebs."

"I'll ... see what I can do."

"Third, before the sun crests that horizon, I want you to get this woman a giant bottle of the best mead in Firestone."

"The moment you show me the Sieve, I'll be off to Mournloff's to ask."

"Fourth, and finally: you go. Now. Back to your estate. If we get the Sieve, we'll bring it to you. Stop following us."

Burgomaster Florin must have figured this to have been a more-than-reasonable price, because he backed out of the clearing, nodding and grinning, until he could be seen no more.

ɪɪ

"The disk. The ring. You can't pull it."

A young boy's voice. It stabbed at Shalm. She shook her head against it. *"How many steps have we taken?"* *"I don't know. I lost track."* *"You lost track?! You will doom us all!"*

"Kneel before the ring," Jayn was saying. " Put your hands upon the disk."

Shalm knelt in the dew-slick grass and put her palms down upon the giant mental disk.

"Trace an 's' with your hand," said the boy.

Shalm did so.

"That's the first letter of your name, mothy!" he said with young delight.

I couldn't count my steps tonight. I can't even track down a single bottle of mead. I cannot do any of the things I'm supposed to do. I couldn't save you. And when I couldn't do that, I couldn't control myself.

Shalm wouldn't cry, but every breath was pain, every heartbeat was pain, every thought was pain.

"You can clasp the ring now," said the boy. "You can lift the lid."

And after I lost you, I was alone.

Shalm wrapped her hands around the iron ring and leaned back upon her knees, pulling hard and grunting with the effort.

I am all alone.

A wail of rust and complaint filled the early morning air.

All alone, Shalm thought.

Then, she felt a hand upon her back. She blinked and looked up to see Jayn looking at her, studying here.

"You're still breathing," Jayn said. "You're still here."

"True words," Shalm said in surprise. "And *you're* still here!"

"Where was I going to go?" Jayn asked.

Boyish laughter rippled faintly on the wind, scattering and diminishing.

Shalm wiped the sweat from her brow and stood. The two women looked at the gaping hole that plunged into the earth before them.

Jayn pulled a length of rope from her robes, and fastened one end around one of the willow trees. She threw the rest of the coil into the shaft and it vanished soundlessly into the depths.

"So that's the ancient sewers of Firestone?" asked Shalm.

"Indeed," said Jayn. "Not quite a myth, but as fierce as one. You have had to endure the visions of the ichor. Would you like me to descend first?"

"Nothing can frighten me now," said Shalm, and swung

herself out into the opening.

The rope was long and sturdy. Shalm descended quickly, occasionally kicking off of the side of the shaft to keep the length unsnagged. Bits of mortar crumbled under her boots, but she never heard them land. She looked up to get a sense of her progress, but the night was so complete overhead that she couldn't see where the shaft opened into the air. Looking down, there was even less to see. An utter absence of light. Receding depths without seeming terminus.

Shalm kept climbing until she reached the end of the rope. Then she lowered herself the last several feet, until her arms were extended far over her head, her hands tight on the frayed rope, and her feet dangling over an unknown emptiness. There wasn't anything left to do except let go or give up.

Shalm let go.

For a long time, she fell, occasionally grazing the rough brick edges of the shaft, and she braced herself for the inevitable impact at the bottom. Instead, she felt herself scraping, more and more, against the side of the shaft, and then sliding along it, and she realized that the shaft had gradually inclined so that its ongoing descent continued at an angle. As the incline increased, an unspoken chthonic pressure, a counterpoint to her downward trajectory, welled up from the depths, and slowed Shalm's descent. A distant skittering sound far above her let her know that Jayn had not forsaken her, and was discovering the depths herself. But Shalm continued down.

Down, down, down, and finally the angle of descent was so slight that Shalm was able to stand upright, and continue walking. The hole had finally become a corridor, round and black, and by reaching out, Shalm was able to touch the slick walls, fuzzy with a dark-loving mold. A trickle of water issued from the cracks in the masonry, and Shalm's feet found a small stream running beneath her now. She continued a bit farther until the tunnel had leveled out entirely, then stood and waited for her friend.

"Shalm?"

When she heard Jayn's voice, it was close, just a few feet away, and tremored with fear for the first time that night.

"It's me," said Shalm. "How far down do you think we are?"

"I don't know. Hundreds of feet, surely. Maybe a thousand."

"We're going to have a devil's time getting out," said Shalm.

"It's a maze down here. But I know that these old sewers connect with the newer somewhere, and if we can find where they join we should be able to eventually get out. After that, you just have to follow the water upstream!"

"We'll need some light if we're going to follow anything. Do you have your lantern?"

"It got smashed on the way down. I'm lucky I didn't slash

my hands."

"That's ill fortune. But wait, I can see something."

As the two felt their way further along the tunnel, it gradually became suffused with an eerie cold light emanating from the molds clinging to the walls and ceiling. The stream thickened and deposited them near a pool where three tunnels converged, each contributing a tributary current that swirled in its basin before tumbling over a stony lip and continuing its journey down a larger fourth tunnel.

"But what will we find downstream?" Shalm asked. "A demon?"

"Perhaps. But we should mark where we've been. So we don't get lost."

Jayn felt around in her robes and produced a small wedge of chalk. She used it to etch a diamond upon the wall of the tunnel they had taken. Then they skirted the pool and rejoined the downward-flowing stream. The current ran strong and cold now, and even Shalm had to keep her hands on the walls to keep from being swept off her feet. The glowing mold stuck to her fingers, and she irritably wiped it off upon her breeches. The leather glowed blue from Shalm's inky fingerprints.

"This isn't poison, is it?" she asked.

"I would assume that everything we find down here is poison," Jayn answered.

The distribution of the mold changed as they went. In

some places, the walls were now bare of the growth, and these made hollow patches so dark that they almost seemed like holes opening into other spaces. Other worlds. Elsewhere, the mold clumped so closely that its light compacted into sere and sickly points, like green stars. Stars that almost gathered. Almost as if ...

"Jayn, is that –"

"The Master Hunter, yes."

"And that –"

"The Howling Bear. The mold mimics the constellations."

"But how is that –"

"I don't know, but I wouldn't study it too closely. We are apt to find many strange things down here, this chthonic realm. We could translate them if we wished, but what madness would befall us then? The mortal mind is only built to absorb a set allotment of reality. It is good to seek out truth, of course, but one must do so provisionally, and with caution. We need our illusions if we are to survive and thrive. Our goals are not deep. You need your mead and I need congratulations. We both need the Sieve. Leave these other truths lying by the side of the road."

But the fungal script was compelling. It was only with great effort that Shalm wrenched her eyes away from the glowing spectacle and focused on following the tunnel onward. Downward.

At length, they arrived at another shaft, five feet across. The water vanished into the earth, but no sound of splashing or impact answered; just the steady churn of motion. While the earlier tunnels had been built of brick and masonry, here the tunnel wormed its way through naked bedrock. Shalm shuddered as a small cavern came into view, furred with stalactites and stalagmites, looming out of the opposite side of the hole.

"We don't want to fall down that," said Jayn.

"Is that where the demon lives?" asked Shalm.

"I think that's where it came from. I think it lives over there." She pointed toward the cave opening. "Regardless, if either of us fell now, I don't think we'd ever return."

"Do you have any more rope?"

"I don't. We'll have to jump."

"I don't like it."

"What are we going to do? We can't go back. We have to go forward."

Since Shalm was hesitating, Jayn took the lead. She got a running start, planted her feet at the edge of the shaft, and launched herself toward the cave entrance. But as she leaped, her feet caught on the hem of her giant robes. Jayn started to pitch into the pit, but her arms just cleared the opposite side. She desperately grabbed for any handhold.

Now Shalm didn't have a choice. Standing on the edge of the hole, she bent her knees and leapt toward the opening. She landed easily on the far side, knelt and grasped Jayn by the hands, and hauled her up again. They both fell in a heap inside the mouth of the cave, panting with relief.

"Let's return another way," said Shalm.

"Indeed," murmured Jayn. She was looking up at the roof of the cave. "That must be its sigil."

The outline of an eye, liquid and baleful, frowned down upon them. Something had cut the image into the mold glowing upon the ceiling.

"Weapons now?" asked Shalm.

Jayn palmed her club. Shalm drew the rusty sword. They got to their feet and made their way deeper into the cavern.

They knew the lair when they arrived.

A great natural room, its roof lost in the shadows overhead, dozens of feet across, and at least a dozen other tunnels radiating out and upward. The two women had found the center and bottom of the ancient sewer system. Heaps of junk and not junk lay in moldering piles across the floor: splintered brooms, smashed crates, crushed pottery, and heaps of dust and ash. But also piles of multi-faceted diamonds, emeralds, and rubies shining like perfectly polished mirrors. Shelves of arcane tomes, both chthonic and empyrean, written in multi-dimensional characters that seemed to project from their opal-bound covers and float in space, illumined by wicked light. Machines of inchoate coordinates, with cardinal parts and capable of restructuring reality when operated by capable recondite hands. And then, in the most obscure corner, a circular sieve, quicksilver wet, forged not in metal and water but in flesh-rendered dreams, shaped in stellar heat by radiating hammers, and woven into its final form by threads of the darkest energy.

"We have found it," breathed Shalm. "But who would leave such a treasure unguarded?"

"It is not unguarded," said Jayn.

"A trap?"

"I don't think so. The Demons of the Roots cannot make traps of their own. Their very existence is a trap. But this creature is here. I feel eyes. It is watching us. I think it is waiting to see if we take anything."

"We have no choice but to confront it or to turn back?"

"None at all."

"Then let's get on with it!"

And with that, Shalm strode across the cavern, her rusty sword gleaming dully in the moldlight, and caught up the Sieve in her other arm.

The demon came upon them instantly. From the unseen depths of the ceiling it fell, and they could not look upon it directly, for it was not of their world. All they recalled afterwards, in the spasms of waking nightmares, was a great mass of hollow eyes, not orbed in flesh but transparent like bubbles, rainbow-hued, agleam, and enveloped in the wings of a giant bodiless, limbless bat.

The demons were not of the world at all but had been

conjured forth from their own strange realms by the ancient invocation of forbidden magic. As prisoners out of time, they did not draw distinctions or hope to negotiate with their captors but strove only to destroy whatever encroached upon their hordes. And here, in a place so deep and dark that it hadn't been molested by mortals in over a thousand years, this winged eyething was consumed by confusion about and hatred of the two mortal women who tried to seize what it had bought.

Its soundless shriek rent their brains and sent them both to their knees, their palms to their ears, their eyes shut against the horror. So Shalm dropped both her sword and the sieve and held her hands to her face just to save herself, for a moment, from the derangement of the creature's impossible appearance. But Jayn recovered more quickly. When she had closed her eyes, she had taken up a rock from the floor and flung it in the direction of the abomination. She imagined its bafflement, for an instant, at this unexpected show of resistance. Then, seizing upon the only defense she could think of – for Jayn knew already that her club would be useless against a creature such as this – she grabbed an armful of precious stones and ran back toward the cavern entrance.

"Creature of the deeps!" she cried, her voice breaking in terror. "Go fetch your trinkets."

And Jayn dumped the gemstones down the gaping hole.

The creature did not fly after them, for these were the least of its treasures. Instead, it descended upon Jayn and enveloped her with its silk-smooth evereyed substance. Jayn fell with a shriek, but the shrieking was in her mind. The creature was invading her brain. It was coating her whole identity and the vault of her memories with an acid of hate and gazing. Its eyes, inward looking, saw through muscle and bone and into Jayn's thoughtstream. First, her present thoughts – befriend Jayn and claim the sieve – then her hidden thoughts – her worthlessness in the visions of the Scrollmasters of Firestone – and finally, her unknown thoughts – desire, rest, security, and dreams – which cannot be named, but whose utterance can only bring forth tears and trembling, for such thoughts comprise a real name. And having found a treasure it craved more than any arcane machine or ancient tomb – a living mind upon which to feed – the eyed bat opened its transparent beak and started to feed upon Jayn's passions and memories.

But its feeding and arrogance had distracted it from the other mortal in its presence.

Shalm saw Jayn wearing the demon like a diaphanous gown and started hurling rocks and gems and books and treasures upon it. These passed through without the creature noticing.

Then Shalm ran up to the feeding demon and stabbed it with her sword at an angle just above the spasming Jayn. The thing blinked its many eyes in annoyance. One eye fixed itself upon Shalm and spoke into her brain in its language of sigils and symbols: *As I prey on her, so will I destroy you too. You cannot keep count, mortal. You cannot number all of the steps you take. You cannot drink to atone for the deeds you have done. No god, no ritual can rescue you. They are not real, and neither are you.*

These words, meant to cow Shalm into paralysis, had the opposite effect. Ghastly and impossible as the demon was, Shalm loathed its words even more. She *needed* her mead, she *needed* to count, she *had* to return to the surface, to some sort of sunrise – to silence in the absence of absolution – and – Shalm gasped – to friendship! Yes, for the first time in years of loneliness, *I have a friend!*

Shalm dropped her rusty sword, and it clattered as it hit the floor.

She drew the wickedly curved dagger and held it above her head.

The iris dilated in the invisible, baleful eye.

Jayn struck it in the middle of its pupil.

The demon shrieked with its horned beak. Shrieked with its bats' wings. Shrieked with its millions of flickering eyes. One eye, alone, had flashed out, but the others all quivered with pain and the realization of their own vulnerability.

Swiping desperately from side to side, Shalm beat the creature back.

It flapped its wings against her, its beak clicked, its claws scraped, and its horrible eyes projected malice and the intention of destruction, but it was an alien life form, and it could not understand that its attacks only drove Shalm into a greater frenzy.

With cuts and plunges and implacable advance, she pushed it back and back, away from Jayn, through the mouth of the cave, and to the very mouth of the hole leading into the ground.

"You cannot have us!" Shalm bellowed and put out the light in three eyes.

With a wheeze of hatred and contempt, the creature wrapped its vast wings about its suppurating mounds of eyes. It fell noiselessly into the pit. It disappeared from view. But Shalm knew, even then, that it would return, better prepared and with reserves of hatred. So she rushed over to her friend.

Jayn was breathing shallowly. Though she was, to all appearances, uninjured, Shalm could sense the injury her friend had suffered. Her memories, emotions, and dreams had been shredded by that fearsome beak and the scrutiny of the horrible eyes. And the acid still clung to her mind, dissolving as it touched. Jayn was being consumed from the mind outward, and if she was not cleansed, she was certain to vanish altogether.

Again, acting on a knowledge she had not learned, Jayn ran back into the cavern and retrieved the Silver Sieve. She placed it gently under Jayn's head. Then, reaching into a pool and returning with water cupped between her palms, Shalm bathed Jayn's face. Each trickle of water washed away the invisible acid. It fell onto the sieve and dissolved into vapor. After three washes, Jayn was breathing calmly again. Another five, and her eyes fluttered open. After Shalm poured water onto her face for the tenth time, Jayn sat up, rubbed her head, and spat into the gloom.

"Well, that is surely the worst nightmare I've ever endured. Did you kill it?"

"I hurt it with my knife. But I did not kill it, and I think it will be returning soon."

"No worries. We can be off now. I think that any of these tunnels here will lead up and connect to the new sewers. It might take a while, but I don't think we'll have any trouble finding our way to the surface again. And we've got the Sieve!"

But dismay answered Jayn's joy:

"I saved you but sacrificed the Sieve," Shalm said.

The invisible acid had utterly melted the sieve. All that remained now were a few bands of silvery wire, twisted and warped.

"I feel that we are very unlucky," said Jayn, "and yet we must be the luckiest animals on this fetid planet. Who could vie with a thing like that yet survive with little injury? That's a miracle, isn't it?"

"Some sort of miracle," murmured Shalm.

"I'm sorry, but please remind me now: what is your name?"

"Call me Shalm," Shalm said.

12

The sun was already high in the sky when the aged beekeeper started to make his way back from the North Gate of Firestone. It had been a long and fog-drenched night, and the sun's brightness notwithstanding, a few stray strands of mist still clung to the earth.

The old man felt similarly veiled. He had passed a restive night, filled with many ill dreams, as had his neighbors. They had all woken in the morning, swimming in sweat, their heads aching. They had dreamed of silent eyes hungrily watching. But when the morning arrived, the dew was on the grass, and the old man thanked the gods for a perfect, blue, sparkling sky.

It had been in these good spirits that he had approached the town guard to beg them for some crusts of bread. In his experience, the guards were usually ill-tempered, but he always gave them a try. At the North Gate, they were often bored and looking for conversation; if he traded them some of his honey, he often came away with breakfast.

Not today.

The guards, still apprehensive of hateful eyes and embarrassed by their cries in the night, had comforted themselves by beating him severely. At least they had left him with his personal stock, though he would have traded all this for a single moldy bit of bread or even a few stray coppers.

"Damn the guard," he muttered as he went. "Damn the birds and the clouds and the sunlight. Damn this day. Damn this cursed city with its cursed water and everyone who lives here, too!"

As if in answer, he heard a heavy grating sound. One of the stone bricks enclosing the chambers of the New Sewer slid roughly to the side, and someone within the aperture swore loudly to themselves.

"It's not so bad," came the light-hearted reply.

"You wouldn't say that if you'd been moving bricks after hours of climbing!"

The beekeeper stared at the opening, holding his breath. Then, to his amazement, two muck-crusted hands appeared on the rim of the hole, and a woman hauled herself out. She was tall, heavy, light-skinned, and strong, with her dark hair swept back in a knot in the style of the Northerners. She was exhausted, covered in mud and a bit of blood. The man slunk back and hid behind a tree. He watched as the woman knelt and reached back into the hole. She lifted out a tiny dark-skinned woman with steel-streaked black hair wearing robes larger than herself. The smaller woman looked just as weary and weathered as the big woman but seemed in much better spirits.

"One night of adventure, my friend, but see, it is day again. And we can rest during the sunlit hours before we go demon hunting again tonight."

"You can have your demons and vampires," said the large

woman. "I am weary beyond words, though I'll regret saying so by tonight. All I want is rest."

"Rest!" said the other. "How can you speak of rest? Today we have threatened the servants of the Lich. Then we threatened the Lich himself. Then we battled that which is greater than the Lich. And we have lived to sing about it!"

This was more than the old man could take. He reached to his belt and pulled forth a flask of his homemade mead. It was sickly sweet and cloying in the humid morning air, but it took his fear from these two subterraneous miscreants with their delusions of grandeur. He stole off again to reunite with his hives down by the river.

13

"It sounds like you found what you were looking for, friend Jayn," said Shalm, wiping her hands on her breeches. Her palms and pants were muddy and her efforts made no difference, but she didn't care.

"Did you keep count as we climbed through the sewers?" asked Jayn.

"Thirteen-thousand, four-hundred-and-fifty-two steps. Many of them vertical. After this, I want to stay in a city with no stairs."

"I cannot help you with that, I am afraid, but I can offer

you a bed today. You may enjoy my goose-feather pillow. I think I'll curl up under the table. I'm so tired, I could sleep on a bed of nails."

"You'd better offer me your bed; I saved your life twice tonight."

"Not just my life, but my sense of hope. Even if my employers won't honor me, you have seen what I can do."

"And you, I."

"We fought the worthy fight. We worked for worthy goals. If we had succeeded, we could have restored safe drinking water to all of Firestone!"

"Instead, we failed and made many enemies. The Lich. Overlord Margate. The Nine Magistrates. Even Burgomaster Florin is going to think we betrayed him somehow."

"And we didn't even succeed in getting you a drink of mead. But worry not. We'll wake by sunset, and then we'll never stop searching until we've won our victory. Not if we have to throttle every magistrate and kick down every door in every district. Not if we have to tangle with a hundred vampires and a thousand demons from beneath. Not if we have to dethrone the Lich himself and take up rule in his stead! Not even if we —"

"Forget it, Jayn," grunted Shalm. "It's Firestone."

ABOUT THE AUTHOR

Photo by Eric Dutro

Connor Coyne is a writer living and working in Flint, Michigan.

He's published several books including the award-winning *Urbantasm* series, and his short work has been featured in *Vox.com*, *Belt Magazine*, and elsewhere. He lives with his wife and two daughters in Flint's College Cultural Neighborhood (aka the East Village), less than a mile from the house where he grew up.

Learn more about Connor's writing at ConnorCoyne.com

www.ingramcontent.com/pod-product-compliance
Lightning Source LLC
Chambersburg PA
CBHW070806120626
46557CB00002B/735